The Last Love Letter

~

Amanda Easton

PublishAmerica
Baltimore

© 2007 by Amanda Easton.
All rights reserved. No part of this book may be reproduced, stored in a retrieval system or transmitted in any form or by any means without the prior written permission of the publishers, except by a reviewer who may quote brief passages in a review to be printed in a newspaper, magazine or journal.

All characters in this book are fictitious, and any resemblance to real persons, living or dead, is coincidental.

First printing

ISBN: 1-4241-9851-8
PUBLISHED BY PUBLISHAMERICA, LLLP
www.publishamerica.com
Baltimore

Printed in the United States of America

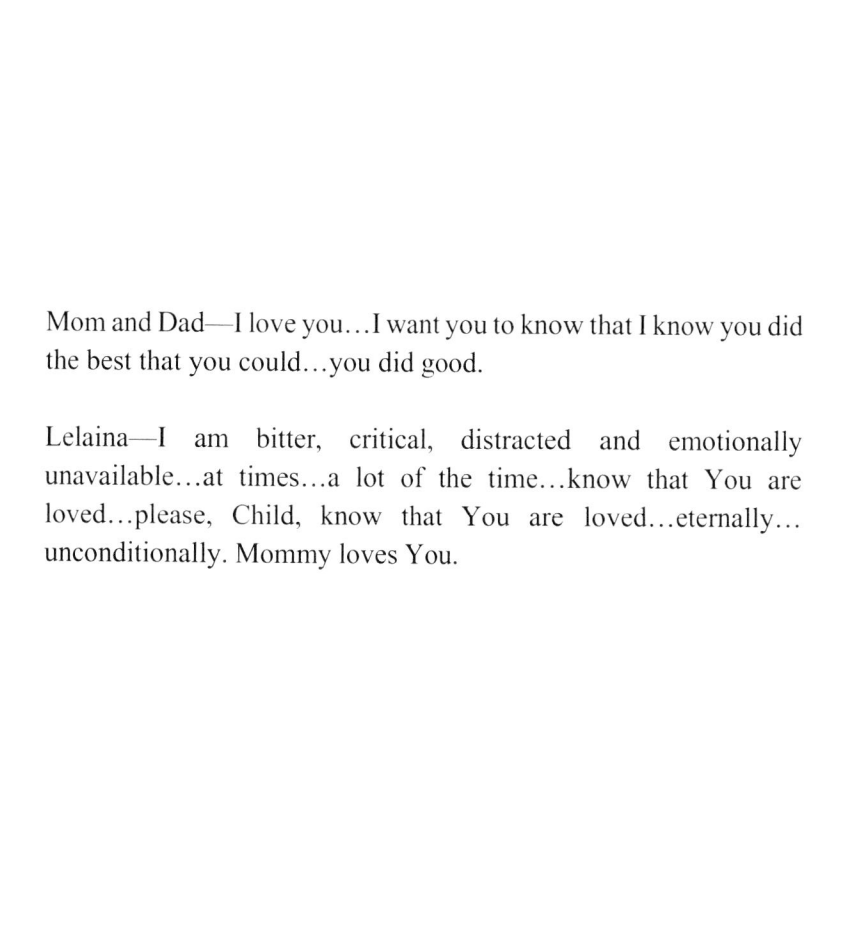

Mom and Dad—I love you…I want you to know that I know you did the best that you could…you did good.

Lelaina—I am bitter, critical, distracted and emotionally unavailable…at times…a lot of the time…know that You are loved…please, Child, know that You are loved…eternally… unconditionally. Mommy loves You.

Acknowledgments

As people grow and mature, some of us have strange, painful relationship experiences, experiences that force us to really take a look in the mirror and quietly acknowledge if we are anything like the person we want to be. And though it's not always the most pleasant experience, reconciling oneself with the enormous gap between what is and what could be, it can be useful. Those moments have value. That's what I've learned as I've matured and grown. I've worked my way through humbling relationships in my life, all of which I've created. Thankfully, I've arrived on the other side, proud to be that person I see in the mirror. For those of you who bravely stood by, for whatever amount of time, and just witnessed my life, without trying to fix me or shut me up because of the pain it provoked in you, I thank you. I didn't need you to carry me or lead me by the hand. I just didn't want to walk alone. Thank you for just being there, at my side. I will always remember you and I wish you well.

To my sister, Carmen Easton—thank you for being there for me and my child over the last five years. We appreciate you, Titi. Same goes for you Grandma and Papa.

Thank you to my mother, Carmen Easton, my sister, little Carmen, Mary Bryant, Cathy McKay and Onica Ziegler for proofing and/or reading my work and giving me feedback. Thank you to everyone who helped me in some way during this process.

Hey Love,

So You're reading this
That's cool

Probably should warn You

Land mines ahead
Rainbows too
Land mines and Rainbows…

Here I am
Outside Your heart

I live here
Outside Your heart

I was listening to a song
Off a CD I made
Behind the wheel of my truck
45 minutes late to work
As usual

It's a song about love
Pretty, little love song
A song about a love that's strong enough
Weathers it all

Insecurity
Jealousy
Competition
Fear
Vanity
Power
Control
Nothing penetrates this love

A fiery love
A fiery love without pride

It's not our song

It's my song
My song about You

Wishful thinking

Yeah
I have songs about You
Still
After all this time

Even new songs about You

No
I don't know why

(I found all these mix tapes I made in college during that time of my life when my every other thought was about You…did You know I had a time in my life when my every other thought was about You? All the tapes I made then were about You too…they have interesting names like "I Only Have to be Perfect" and "She's No Competition")

I was doing alright
Or so I thought
I was breathing anyway
Being

It had been almost three years
Since I last saw Your face

12 days shy of three years

THE LAST LOVE LETTER

Yes
I remember
To the day

Three years after I sent The Letter

God
That Letter

You know
I wince
I cringe
When I think of it
Every time

The Letter

I have flashbacks
Every so often
They take me by surprise

That Letter

I wrote it
I proofed it
I sent it

And I have never been able
To read it again

Never

I tried to find a copy of it the other day
I couldn't

Thank God

It's the same with that poem
I wrote for You in college

They're too much
Both of them

Too much

I know

I don't really blame You
For not responding to The Letter

What does one say to a letter like that?
Who knows…

I got a letter like that once
Well, I think
It's *possible* I got a letter like that once

A letter from someone
Who felt way too much

Unjustified feelings

A person who had minimal impact
On me
In the scheme of things

THE LAST LOVE LETTER

Who didn't compel in me an iota of feeling
Not good feeling anyway

I remember being annoyed
Mildly annoyed
Most of the time

Very annoyed
Some of the time

All that unjustified feeling
Unreasonable
Illogical
Dramatic
Stupid
Weak
Indicative of some deep-seeded issue
Some unnamed need

And not my problem

I threw that letter in the garbage
Yep
After only reading the first paragraph

One last vain attempt
Win my heart
Win my compassion
Futile

And just too much

Maybe that's what happened to The Letter
My Letter
Maybe You threw That Letter in the garbage
After only reading the first paragraph

Maybe You never got to That Part in The Letter

That should give me relief

It doesn't

On second thought
I do blame You
I do

Maybe it's vanity
(I'm sure it's vanity)
But I'm feeling
Like
Since I wrote That Letter
And it took
Every ounce of courage
I could muster
To send You
That Goddamn Letter
You should have read it

A couple of times
In fact

Let's say
You read it
The Letter

THE LAST LOVE LETTER

And
You didn't respond

Which is
Undeniably
A response

Honestly
It was probably two months
Before I stopped checking my caller ID
Every day
As soon as I got home
To see if You called

60 days or so
Doing the same thing
Checking my caller ID

60 days

Hoping for some small piece of validation
Some acknowledgment
That You got
The Letter

My last vain attempt

60 days
Every day

Gets to be a habit
Sad, little habit

Then it sunk in
Finally
Late one summer night

You hadn't responded
Because
You weren't going to

Ever

Like all those phone calls in college
You requested
And just ignored

By the way
I have NEVER
In my WHOLE life
ASKED someone to call me
Knowing
I had NO intention
Of ever returning the phone call
What's the point of that?
WHAT IS THE POINT TO THAT?

unfuckingbelievable

Got rid of my land line
Altogether
Trying to break that sad, little habit

THE LAST LOVE LETTER

Stopped putting myself
In a time and space
Where You could request
My phone calls
You'd just ignore

Fast forward
Three years

Was doing alright
Or so I thought
Breathing
Just being

Getting up in the morning
Dragging myself into work

Loving my child
With what's left
Of my shattered, little heart

Moving forward
I hoped

Working out again
Running over my lunch hour
Had stopped getting high too
Eating pretty well
(Except for the Oreo cookie fluff, Brach's Bridge Mix and Better
Batter ice cream…well basically eating well)

Getting my shape back

Started thinking about love again
That's what one does
They say

Get back on the horse

Wasn't thinking about "doing" love again
Fuck that
No interest in the doing part
No interest in dating
Or the getting-to-know-ya stuff
Too labor-intensive
That whole process

Would need a babysitter
Too
For my mini-me

Not into babysitters
For my mini-me

She's just better off with me
Mini and me
Safe

And all that
Would require a clean house
Too

THE LAST LOVE LETTER

Clean house is a low priority
As of late

Just not in the mood
Actually
To get back on the horse

Not right now

Thought I'd walk
Meander
And think about You
For a while

Sort myself out

I was remembering
At first
Kisses

I was remembering kisses

I don't remember many kisses
Except the bad ones
Burned on the brain
All those awful kisses

Like that guy who bit the area under my nose
Trying to swallow my face
Chomp

Horrible kiss

Or Kale's itty bitty teeny weenie
"My feelings for you are little and slight
Hence the little, slight kisses" kisses
(I was told he once complained to a mutual friend that I kissed too hard…it's called passion…alien concept…I'm sure…for the love 'em and leave 'em crowd)

I remember the really good ones too

Like that caramel boy's kisses
The "you're so pretty to me" kisses
Loved those kisses
Felt *elegant*
Desired
After those kisses

Other kisses
Regular kisses
Average kisses

All those kisses without depth or feeling
Obligatory kisses
Thanks for dinner and goodnight
No, you're not coming up kisses on the cheek

Those kisses just fade away

I don't remember Your kisses

Wait
There was that one

THE LAST LOVE LETTER

Your face was so close to mine
I was breathing hard
You were on top
Inside of me

You kissed me

Surprised me
That kiss
Cuz I remember
You were pretty pissed

First pretty pissed
Then a kiss

Surprising

That was the night
You let me come home with You
From the bar

Cuz my ride left without me

I had been sitting in Your car
For 45 minutes
Talking to You

About some bullshit

I had no place to go
Certainly no means of getting there
You asked me
What was I planning to do next?

Not, "So, do you want to come home with me?"
No
Just, "What are you going to do now?"

"What are you going to do now?"
So that I had to *ask* to come home with You

Because
You know
That's easy
Asking Someone
To let you come home with Them
When it's 2:30 in the goddamn morning
You're sitting in Their car
You have no way of getting home
And They didn't seem to think to invite you first

I was very practiced at that
Wouldn't Ya think?
Suggesting that men take me home
Unwillingly
Because I can't afford the cab ride back to Ames
As a college kid
And calling one of my friends
In the middle of the night
To make an 1 ½ hour trip to and from Des Moines
Cuz I missed my ride
Talking to That Guy
Who tried to fuck My DiDi Baby
Just seemed…
Oh, I don't know…

Inappropriate

"Please take me home with You"
Yeah
Easy peasy
Lemon squeezy
Cuz I'm very practiced at that

I got snappy
Wasn't the most mature response
I know
(Still feelin' kind of snappy about it…though)

Maybe You had plans
Or maybe You were just tired
Didn't want company
Maybe Your house was messy
Or on fire
I can relate…totally

But
I was kind of ass out that night
And You knew it
Being cool
That would have been alright too

Pretty pissy
You were

Having to take me home from the bar
And fuck me
What a pain in the ass
I feel Ya

I cleaned Your house
Next morning
While You were at work
Waiting for my ride

My olive branch

Right now remembering
You didn't even call to thank me

You walked in
Your house was different from when You left
Clean
You didn't pick up the phone
To say "Thank you"

"Thank you"
A Perfectly Natural Response
A Good Person
Would have to suppress
Under such circumstances

If they appreciated another
If

But You did
Graciously
Let me sleep there
That night
Guess we're Even-Stevens

And I wasn't trying to "hog" the bed
For the record

THE LAST LOVE LETTER

Just wanted to cuddle with You
Lay with You
After the sex
Remember the sex?

Approached it sly-like
Like I just happened to end up
On Your side of the bed
Maybe I'll just put my arm around You
That could be comfortable

Cautious
Cuz You were pissy

Pretty pissy
You were

The usual

You accused me of being a "bed hog"
When in reality
My problem was
I'm just not that confident
Handling passive-aggressiveness
After sex

Excusez moi

I responded with something mean
Something about all the other girls
Knowing the routine

Giving up the ass
And then staying
On their side of the bed

Forgive me
My bad

Tit for tat

Yeah
It's all comin' back

Before that
There was the Sneaky Kiss

After the bar in Ames
And that godforsaken drive down to Des Moines
Sitting next to our respective friends
On Your couch
In Your new apartment
On Kingman

The Sneaky Kiss

The You-shushed-me-for-kissing-too-loudly kiss
And the fuckin' shush was louder than the kiss

I remember what it was like to kiss You
I remember

Wondering if You ever kissed me back
Can't recall

THE LAST LOVE LETTER

All my hungry kisses
I remember

Burned on the brain
All those hungry kisses

And You

Oh yeah
Remembering the Friday make-out session
Right before You broke Your ankle
Right before I went to Puerto Rico

There was one kiss in particular
I remember
I savored that kiss
Me kissing You
Yet again

I remember looking down
Into Your glorious face
Kissing Your lower lip
Softly

That was our last time together
Summer 2000
Didn't realize it would be the last time
It was

I called You the next day
Unafraid
Thought it would be ok

You'd be sweet
No doubt
Cuz I gave good love
The night before
Left a message

You never did call back

Weeks later
Visited a medium on a farm
In Michigan
Her name was June
Old lady, like 70-something

June
The Psychic

I asked her about You
She said there was a girl
(Well, she said there were lots of girls, actually)

But one
In particular
Not Your wife
Almost
You treated her as if
That was her Intended Place in Your life
June said

News to me

THE LAST LOVE LETTER

June said
You did care about me
When I asked

"In His own way"
Is what she said

Not sure what that meant
And I was too scared to get clarification

Didn't help
When she added
I wanted to be loved
So badly
I settled

Makes
"In His own way"
Sound
Well
Like
"Not much"

Advised I leave You alone
June did
"Give Him wide berth"
Her words
Exactly

Later
You told me
You moved in with Your son's mother
You were engaged too

That stung

Don't know why though
I had been warned
By June
The Psychic

You told me that You and she were not together
You told me that You didn't love her
Not like that

Granted
You did qualify that statement with
"Well, not right now"

But still

You might want to choose
Your words
More carefully
More truthfully
When discussing such things
With love sick puppies

You knew
That's what kills me
When I look back on it
You knew

You knew
Telling me the truth
Would end it

THE LAST LOVE LETTER

You and I
Were nothing
We would never be anything
You had plans

You lied
You omitted things
Misrepresented
You lied

And I don't know why
I don't understand why

I never got the feeling You really liked me
Not in any way that mattered
What difference would it have made
If it had stopped?

If we had just stopped
What difference would it have made?

What would it have changed in Your life?
Not fucking me once every blue moon?
So what?

There was a line
I could have taken a number
And gotten in line
When it came to You

Silly broads
Looking me up and down
At The Club
Sizing me up
Little did they know
I was no competition
I wasn't their competition
Not when it came to You

I was nobody
When it came to You

There was a line

You could have picked anyone else
Any random snow bunny at The Club
Replaced me easily
Effortlessly
My tiny, temporary space in Your life
One night
One insignificant night every blue moon
Could have been anyone
Literally anyone
Warming their side of Your bed
Anyone else

Why would it have mattered
If I let go?

I never understood

THE LAST LOVE LETTER

There were people
Then
Who liked me
Too much
I knew

And I was very clear
I didn't feel the same
No wiggle room
I didn't feel the same

I stopped fucking with them
As soon as I realized
It caused them pain
Cuz their pain
Annoyed me
Cuz I didn't feel the same

And all that shouting
And whining
All that drama
Made the sex not fun

It was about a thing
Some shit to do
To pass the time
While thinking of You

I didn't feel the same
And they knew

I made sure
They knew

You
You requested phone calls
You later avoided
Or just couldn't be bothered to return
How courageous

I've got a book
Provides the psychological motivation
For attracting a bodily injury
Says
Broken ankle =
Guilt over receiving pleasure

Totally avoidable
You and I
If you had chosen
Your words
More carefully
More truthfully

I might have broken a few hearts
In college
Including my own
But I didn't break any ankles

I heard June
Heard that You were not for me
But I didn't listen
You were so beautiful
And charming
When You wanted to be

THE LAST LOVE LETTER

One last vain attempt
Nine years after we met
(For the second time)
I haven't a clue why

What was I trying to accomplish
With
The Letter?

God
That Letter

Then
Not surprisingly
No reply

And no sane options left

Took June's advice
As if I had a choice
Everyone's advice
Actually
And complied with Your unspoken wish

Finally
After nine-plus years
Of plotting
Strategizing
Agonizing

With minimal impact
On You
In the scheme of things

Let it alone
Finally
Gave it a rest

Three years
Of breathing
And just being
Regrouped

Working at my "dream job"
That "big" job I always wanted
Remember?

Totally unmotivated
Ungrateful
Restless

I'm a mom now
Overwhelmed
By the enormous responsibility
Of being someone's whole world
Holding Her self-esteem, self-image, self-worth
In my hands

My shaky hands

She's so beautiful
My Child
And fragile

And I
I'm like a bull in a china shop

THE LAST LOVE LETTER

My life
Is
Unrecognizable

Completely off the map

I work
Grudgingly
And with little satisfaction

I mother
With guilt
And so much trepidation

And I think of You

Still

Everyday
But in a different way
I guess

Without hope
Just regret
And hatred
At times

A lot of the time

You are
No longer
My sweet escape

Then
There You were
All of a sudden

Driving a black car
On 63rd Street
7:40 A.M.
Going to work
I assume

And the color returned
To my little, dead world
Just like that

That moment
So vivid
You
In Technicolor
The whole world was just background
Black and white

First time
In months
I had left on time for work

And there You were
Like a reward
From Heaven

God smiled down on me
For the first time
In three years

THE LAST LOVE LETTER

There You were

Grinning and waving at me
Like You were a Superstar
And I Your fan

It's cool
I am a fan

Die hard
I guess

Cuz this doesn't go away
It doesn't end
It's weird
I know

It's been long enough
Hadn't even seen Your face
Outside of my mind's eye
In three years
Had begun to lose the details

Your exquisite face

I took a relationship psych class in college
The Psychology of Love and Relating
Takes three years to get over losing someone
That's what the book said

Apparently not

I think they have to die
The object of one's affection
For that to be true

Unrequited love
How long does it take to get over that?
12 years and counting…

To be honest
Time hasn't taken much of an edge off this
Not much at all

What is this?!?!?!

There You were
For the first time in three years

And here I am

Feeling the same thing
All over again

My world
Revolves around You
Again

63rd Street
Is a road of possibilities
Opportunity
And You
You are in
Every black car

THE LAST LOVE LETTER

Today is Monday
Tomorrow is Friday
When will I see You again?
What will I be wearing?

I feel like a seventh-grader
Passin' that cute boy in the hall
I'm giddy
It's so exciting
Thrilling
Terrifying
And time flies

Been two months
Since that morning
Today is Your birthday
You're 35 today
It's a big one
35
Wonder how You feel
What You're doin'

Part of me wants to call
Your birthday
The perfect excuse
Happy Birthday, Babe!

I see it
How it plays out
In my head

I get Your phone number
You know I can
I have access

I call

I say "Hey"
You say, "What's up, girl?"
You know it's me
Right off
You recognize my voice

Wait
No
No
No

Remembering that time
I called
So excited
Trying to connect
You said
The conversation
Was blowing Your high

Yeah
Calling
Just lost the taste for it

It would be awkward
And unappreciated

THE LAST LOVE LETTER

Yes
Focus

It would be awkward and unappreciated

No
I won't call

Life is just simpler
Without such things

I'll be smarter about it
This time
Do it from a distance
I'll love You from a distance

And celebrate Your birthday in my head
Happy Birthday, Babe

I have moments
When I want to let go
I mean
Damn
I'm already halfway there

I live my life
In Your birthplace
In Your hometown
And You are nowhere
Nowhere around
But in my head

In my head
You are everywhere
Everywhere

I'm here
Outside Your heart
I live here

You live in mine
In my heart
In my head
All the time

I pretend
I have
Forgotten about You

Sometimes people ask
And I pretend

It's not true
But nevertheless
I pretend
It's just what I do

I want to let go
I try
I do
I swear

Would make perfect sense
Just let go

THE LAST LOVE LETTER

I don't know why
I can't

I've heard
You don't really let anything go
You've ever truly wanted
Until you've loved it
Honored it
Done right by it

It's a problem

I don't have two good thoughts
About You
Together
In a row

So You know

Wish I did
God
I wish I did

The bad ones always intrude
Always

I cannot justify
My feelings
To myself

I cannot justify loving You

And then
Of course
There's the regret
If I had only…

Regret
That's where it gets tricky
Sticky

Things would be different
I suppose
If I could just put
Two good thoughts
About You
Together
In a row

But I don't

Always these moments
Hard moments
Ugly moments
Filled with ugly memories
Of You

Like that one time
You woke me up in the morning
By accidentally elbowing me in my head

You hit me hard enough
To wake us both up

THE LAST LOVE LETTER

And then
You
Opted
Not to say
"Sorry"

I guess
Because
You could

It *was* Your bed

That's not one I think about very often actually

For fear
Of **LOATHING** You

"I'm sorry"
A Perfectly Natural Response
Any GOOD Person
Would have to suppress

If they hit someone "accidentally"
If

That was the morning after the night
I asked to borrow a pen
And You threw a pencil at me
That hit me in my chest

In front of my friend

Though I was sitting
Close enough
You could have just handed it to me
If You had wanted to

In my mind
I go back to that night
To that moment

After the pencil hits me

I pause

I think about how much hostility
You have toward me
Right then

And always

I think about what little
Tenderness, affection, or consideration
You ever really showed me

Especially in comparison to the others
The fucking others

And I consider the consequence
Of rewarding Your conduct
With cuddles and sex

In my mind
I pick up Your pencil
Hand it back to You

THE LAST LOVE LETTER

I say goodbye to You
My Love
Forever

Abrupt
I know

But certainly more DIGNIFIED
And demanding of RESPECT
Than staying the night with You
After You hit me
With a pencil in my chest

I just had a thought

Last time I saw You
First time in three years
Driving a black car
On 63rd Street
7:40 A.M.
Going to work
I assume

My smile was huge
Huge

Because I couldn't help myself

There You were
My Beloved
In all Your glory

There You were

Grinning and waving at me
Not mad at me anymore
Like a dream

Wonder how big
That smile
Will be
Next time

Too easy to smile
For You
My Love

Until I think about getting elbowed in the head

Almost makes me want to rewind
Take that smile back

Rewind
And take all my smiles back

Remembering
The Girls
Girls
Girls
Girls

Some of them
(Most notably)
My dearest friends

THE LAST LOVE LETTER

So many moments
Your behavior
Killed me
Just killed me

I wished we'd never met

Sometimes
I wish we never met

Felt like looking down on You
In those moments
The way You often looked down on me

But they were just moments
Moments that always passed

The pull was still there
You
This Irresistible Magnet
And I
Like a moth to a flame
But very consciously aware
I was dousing myself with gasoline
Gasoline-soaked moth
Hurling toward the flame
The flame and destruction

And I go
Knowing I'll be burned
Badly
Quickly

Knowing I'll explode
I go

I've tried to forgive
(Still tryin')

Hard to forget
(That's never gonna happen)

Flashbacks
Those moments
They catch me
Like a monster
In a nightmare
I can't outrun

I push them back
Wave my hands
Go to my happy place
Dance

Ok
Ok
Ok
I'm ok

Smile
Smile!
Smile!!
Smile!!!

THE LAST LOVE LETTER

Think of something else
Think of something pretty
Something pretty
Maybe something funny

People are watching
PEOPLE ARE WATCHING

DANCE!!!!

Finally
Ok
Ok

We're ok

The moment passes

Sometimes

Sometimes
It's like that

Other times
Not so lucky

Tear-soaked face
Sitting at my desk
At work

My "dream job"
That "big" job I always wanted

Not workin'
Nope

Just sitting at my desk

Wishing I had loved me enough
To stop fucking with You

Loving me enough
There's the work that's left to do

Remembering Stevie now
You remember?
My Tall, Yellow friend?
Don't You?
The one
Who was so flirtatious with You
That night at the club?
'Member?

In front of me

Tried to ignore it
I remember thinking
He would never
Not with Stevie
Not with slutty-ass Stevie

Last night out on the town with Stevie
Fuckin' whore
Made a Mental Note

THE LAST LOVE LETTER

Good old Stevie
The Conductor
A nickname she *earned* in college
Stevie's Love Train
All Aboard

My friend

Hadn't held it against her
To each her own
We were young
18, 19, 20
(not quite 21….at The Club…shhhhh)

We all just wanted to live in Love's Light

Sometimes
Leads to poor judgment
Reaching for the Light
I know

Any condemnation
On my part
Of The Conductor
For being a lustful creature
Could be filed under
Pot and Kettle

I was no butterfly
When I was 18, 19, or 20

'Magine that

So I invited Miss Stevie
Into my glass house
Into my life
And showed her pictures of You
My Beloved

Not realizing
Stupid me

That I had planted an itch
She'd want You to scratch

Then

Then I held it against her

And You
You seemed
Very
Put
Off
By her behavior
That night

Flirting with You
In my face

Disgusted
You seemed

And I took solace in that

THE LAST LOVE LETTER

Too Kingly
My Love

Stevie
Darling
He's much too Kingly for tramps

Then
The next weekend
When she came down to Des Moines
Without me

She told me

Later

You sent over a drink

You sent over a drink

Your Righteous Indignation was
Just
An
Act

She told me
You sent her a drink

Lost Your Crown that day
Baby Boy
So You know

Not quite sure why I put it back

Then
There was Diane
Again
My friend
My best friend

My DiDi Baby
Yellow too
But not so tall

The girl who introduced us
In a parking lot
A year before You remember meeting me
I remember meeting You

She dated Your best friend
'Member?

She told me
Just let the whole thing go

She said
You were just …
What was the word she used?
regular

That's right
You were regular

THE LAST LOVE LETTER

Hadn't I noticed?
She knew You
From him
Your best friend

I must not have known You
Ever
Not really anyway
Otherwise
I would have known too

Known about Your "regularness"

Trust her
Best to wrap my fantasies
Around another
She said

Someone more like me
And less like You

Cuz You were regular
No doubt

No doubt about that

Seemed an ill-fit
At the time
That word
"regular"

AMANDA EASTON

Used to describe My Love
My King
So high up
On Your Pedestal

regular

Thought about it

Thought about how I shielded my eyes
From Your sunshine
Magnificent
You were
So Bright

You were *so* bright

Thought about how I strained my neck
Looking up at You
My King
So high up
You were

You were *so* high

I placed You on that pedestal
Had to lift You up there
Cuz in reality
You're a good inch shorter than me
In all respects

regular

THE LAST LOVE LETTER

And I am not
regular
That is

I've never worn
Nor have I ever aspired to wear
"regular"
Emblazoned across my chest

Sure
It might endear me to the masses

The uninspired masses

But I don't give a fuck about them

Seems that's Your job

Always thought
You hid most of Your sunshine
To be liked more
By them

You tried to be regular
So that You weren't so threatening
To them

So that You were easier to digest
Gain acceptance
From them

Lesser mortals

But maybe
I was wrong

Happened
From time to time
When it came to You

Maybe
Just maybe
My DiDi Baby was right

You
Were
Indeed
regular

And me
Not so much

And it would never work
She said

You saw us walk into The Club together
That Night
My DiDi Baby and I
You knew she was there with me
My friend

I saw You wrap Your arm around her waist
You were talking to her
Looking right into her eyes
I saw You pull her close

THE LAST LOVE LETTER

you both were smiling
you two had a moment

You had a moment
With My DiDi Baby

You made me lean in
Scream whatever I had to say in the bar
As You looked away
Distracted
More concerned about others watching
Than anything I had to say
You didn't close the distance
You didn't smile
I didn't get Your undivided attention
Like my best friend
You didn't wrap Your arms around me
You didn't make it easy
Flirty
Fun

You humbled me

me
The one You *were* sleeping with

We never had discrete conversations
When the cute girls were around
Or Her
God forbid

Can't imagine
You leaning in close
To hear what I had to say
In front of Her
In front of them

Can't recall
Even one occasion
In public
When You touched my waist
Without looking me up and down
To let me know
It was time to play

I was never good enough
Never
No matter what I did

Never
Good
Enough

God forbid
Someone get the impression
That maybe
Maybe
You liked me

You
Regal, Kingly

me
stupid flighty slut

THE LAST LOVE LETTER

Shudder
The thought

I used to think
During nights at The Club
That fuckin' club

When You had words for Everyone
For Anyone
But me

When You'd dance with me
And turn Your back

Your back to me
During our dance

Why?
So You didn't have to look at me?
Or touch me?
Or acknowledge that I was there?
In front of Her?
Was that it?

I don't understand

Then why agree to the dance at all?
Why not just say no?
If no was how You felt

NO WAS HOW YOU FELT

Why not just say "no thank you"?
That would have made the point
Don't You think?

I remember saying "no" to You
When I was too fucking pissed to dance

I used to think
I wonder
How surprised they'd be
All of them
How surprised She'd be
To know
There are times
When He and I are alone
He lays His pretty little head
On my chest and in my lap
Like I was Mary
And He
The Baby Jesus

He falls asleep
On my chest and in my lap

Beneath You then too
But in a different way
I guess

God
It burns
It burns
It burns

THE LAST LOVE LETTER

Ok
Ok
Ok
I'm ok

I saw You call her over to the car
My DiDi Baby
When we were leaving

She told me You asked if WE
She and I
Plural
Could come by

Later
Much later
Actually at her wedding
She told me The Truth

You asked if she
My DiDi Baby
Singular
Could come by

Just her
And leave me behind

No rules
It seems
For Your behavior
No rules

Free for all
No one too sacred
No lines that shan't be crossed

Heavy penalties
Cruelty
For me
When I fuck up

And give my love
Momentarily
To a stranger
Who
While dancing with me
Doesn't turn his back

I suffer
When I fuck up

Later
You said
You propositioned
My DiDi Baby

And I was right there
Smiling
Hoping to God everything was ok

Because You were mad
Mad at me

'Magine that

THE LAST LOVE LETTER

And I listened
To every fucking absurd word
In Your car
For 45 minutes
And missed my ride home

You did it
To be
Vindictive
You said

I AM
Jealous-hearted
Intense
Obsessive
Possessive
Observant
Perceptive
Suspicious
And
Unfortunately Naïve
(horribly naïve…when it comes to spoken words from a loved one…tell me anything…if it sounds good…I'll try and believe)

I AM
Vicious
And
Vengeful
Shy
Aggressive
Real
Phony

Scared
Courageous
Angry
Gentle
Bold
Timid
Sensitive
Abrasive
Truthful
Deceitful
Up-front
Manipulative
Loving
Cold
And
Thin-Skinned
Soft-Hearted
Under My Armor

When crossed
I hurt
I do

Then
I plot
And plan

Hell Hath No Fury

I AM
The very definition of
VINDICTIVE

THE LAST LOVE LETTER

And yet
There's that line

The line
You
Don't
Cross
If
Someone
Means
Anything
To
You

Fucking my friends would be the line
Maybe You weren't aware

And I'm a shitty bitch
When I'm pissed
I know
The Shittiest Bitch of The Bunch

So I would do things
In Front of You
In Your Face

Action Intended To Illicit a Reaction
A Negative Reaction
From You

My Beloved

Things Done to Hurt You

See
Because
If You didn't care
You couldn't be hurt

We both knew
You already had Your Lois Lane

Wondered though
What it would take
To be Your kryptonite?
My Superman

She makes You go weak
That
I can see

I could make You feel weak
Small
Unimportant
I think
Let us try

You felt something
Don't quite know what it was
Not sure if "care" is the right word
But it was something

Spiteful
I AM

But I Never
Ever
Propositioned
One of Your friends
Never
(And it was a little easier for me…never…ever…being attracted to any of Your friends…I know…my friends were pretty cute…STILL THOUGH)

I wouldn't have
No matter what
Out of LOVE and RESPECT
For You

Cuz there's that line

Or so I thought

I know

Stupid me

Despite what You said
Can't help but think
You just wanted to fuck My DiDi Baby

Probably always did

Seeing her
With Your best friend
Cool girl
Pretty girl

Cool, pretty girl
You hadn't fucked yet
Rare
I'm sure

A challenge

Might have already had her
If You had moved more quickly
That first time
Tick tock

Here's Your second chance
She's here

And with Amanda
Her best friend

Fuck it

All is fair
In love and war

Later
If You decide
You know
On a whim
That You might want to fuck me again
You could just tell me
It was my fault

Too easy to manipulate me
Silly me

THE LAST LOVE LETTER

Who so desperately wanted to hear something
Anything that sounded better than
Spending one night
Trying to fuck
My little yellow
Not-so-tall
And very best friend
Would be worth
The Tidal Wave of Disappointment
Crashing over me

Drowning me

Ok
Ok
Ok
I'm ok

You don't want me to love You anymore
Ok

Wish I could say that I loved her the same
My DiDi Baby
After that

But I can't

Tried to put it behind us
Problem was
She was always so fuckin' competitive
Whoever I liked
Magically became more attractive
And she was so attentive

Happened before
It would happen again

Tried to
Love Her
In the Same Way

Went through the motions
Stood up at her wedding
Maid of honor
The best friend

Thanked her for telling me
'Bout You
No problem
Thanked her for having my back

And lost that lovin' feeling

Something broke
Being measured against her
My DiDi Baby
In Your eyes

And coming up short

My DiDi Baby
Just basking
In the sublime rays of Your sunshine
That night

THE LAST LOVE LETTER

Toasty feeling
To be preferred by You
Over me

Red-hot feelin'
I'll bet

Happened
Every once in a while
Every once in a while
She'd have her moment

Dazzling Rays of Your Sunshine
That night
Like a spotlight
The Winner

I get it

We all need a little sunshine

My DiDi Baby
Burnt and Broken

Then
There was Magdalena
My Maggie
Gentle Lunatic
Another love of mine

My Maggie
The Walking Wounded
Too gentle to live amongst the wolves of the world

I, at times, am also a wolf in sheep's clothing
And a sheep
And a shepherd

My Maggie
One of my flock
My Gorgeous Wounded Nutter

Kept her close
She had to be watched
Had that tendency
Of letting the cheese
Slip off the cracker

In The Bell Jar
She was
At times

Told You she was my cousin
(That was a lie)
Hoped it would illicit some loyalty from You

Maybe You'd stop licking Your lips
Salivating

To Your credit
You were a lot smoother 'bout that one
Suave even

Asking me to introduce her to You
So interested in me
You just *had* to meet my friends

THE LAST LOVE LETTER

'Cept
The panting gave You away

Calling me for the first time
In months
Asking about her
Minutes into the conversation
Masterful
Really

If I were a dumb girl
Wouldn't have even noticed
Swear to God
It was *that* Smooth and Genuine

Wish I were dumb

Easier
I think
Life
Would have to be

Happy Little Carrot
Just bouncing 'round
Whorin'
Without a thought in my head

dumb girl
The bliss

I can only imagine
Cuz I'm just not dumb

Yeah
I'll be sure to mention to her You said hi
Hell
Did You want me to call her on three-way for You?
I don't mind hanging up after she answers
Give you two some privacy

I'll step aside

You don't want me to love You anymore
Ok

I'll step aside

Maybe
You and I
Can share a dance
Few months down the road
When You're bored
With that one

Or she snaps and kills Your parents

My Gorgeous Wounded Nutter

Because EVERYTHING
EVERYTHING
About the way I carry myself
Didn't You notice?
Little, insecure, needy and forgiving me
Would suggest that You
Fucking one of my best friends

THE LAST LOVE LETTER

Wouldn't signify the end of our
What shall I call it?
Extended One Night Stand

I had a dream
The other night
About you two

A nightmare

I was pleading with You
Screaming at her
Pulling her hair

My Maggie
Wish I could say she would never
Not with You

Too much love and respect for me
The shepherd
Her shepherd

Don't know though
For sure

Cuz when it comes to dick
Seems I don't have that many friends

Of course
There were more
But I've blocked out
Their names

And I just chalked them up
To The Game
To The Game
To The Game

And played a couple of rounds myself
Just to even the score

No thrill in the kill though
Didn't feel much like winning at all

Kissing him
That blue-eyed Dominican boy
In front of You
And watching You
Turn Your face away from me

Turn Your heart away from me

Well

Didn't exactly inspire a victory dance

The feelings
Must have been different
For You

Must have

As You seemed
To Relish
Your victories

THE LAST LOVE LETTER

Over me

Watching You
Kiss the frizzy-haired girl
In Response
It seemed
The timing
Was sooooo
Suspect
(Probably just more vanity on my part…that interpretation…of that event…but maybe not)

Then there was the empty condom wrapper
Sitting on Your coffee table
In plain sight
The next day
When I stopped by

The whole house was clean
It was a fuckin' miracle
Except for the empty condom wrapper
Sitting on Your coffee table
In plain sight

You
The Winner
The Winner by a landslide
(Never fucked The Dominican…by the way)

What was I?
What was I to You?

Like a toy
Abandoned in a closet
Neglected on some shelf
Forgotten
Until someone else
Wanted to play
With me
What was I supposed to do?
Say no?
And wait for You?
For what?
Me, You and Lois Lane?

I did it wrong
In the beginning
Did You wrong
From the beginning
I know

I think about it all the time
Kick myself in the ass

I should not have fucked You
That first night
I know

I'm not entirely stupid

My Dad gave me the "free milk" speech
(Hmmm…my Dad…probably not…maybe it was one of my friends in college? Regardless…*someone* gave me the "free milk" speech)

THE LAST LOVE LETTER

Bad idea
I know

Gave You the impression
Getting in my pants
Was pretty easy

For You
Admittedly
It Was

But
You are not like everyone
Actually

And maybe I didn't tell You this enough

You are not like any of them
All those completely forgettable boys I met

Unless You really, really try
In an effort to endear Yourself to the masses

Lesser Mortals

You assumed
Cuz it was easy for You
Getting in my pants
Must be easy for others

You underestimated
You
My King

It's funny how we do that

In reality
Never been Dick Crazy
Have known girls who were
Never been

Truth is
I push my buttons
Better than anyone
Has ever pushed my buttons
Ever
I alone

And everyone
Anyone
Is great
In bed
In my head

Even better than the real thing

So dick
Dick holds very little sway over me

But
I dropped my drawers pretty quickly
For You
This is true
Why?
You ask

THE LAST LOVE LETTER

Because I wanted to
There wasn't a moment's hesitation
I wanted to

You were gorgeous
Breathtaking
So beautiful
To me
Then

You still are
So beautiful
To me

I have fantasies
About my Perfect Guy
He has Your face
Your body
He looks like You
Just like You

You were
That first night
Everything

Witty
Funny
Clever
Sharp as a tack

You lived in two worlds
Street *and* Refined
Like a mix between a wolf and a Burmese cat

AMANDA EASTON

Vulnerable and Guarded

Open and Impenetrable

Generous With Praise and Justifiably Critical

Spontaneous and Conservative

Regal and Humble

Personable and Precious

Vain and Deserving

Intoxicating

Like a breath of fresh air

You were
A Breath of Fresh Air

And I opened the window
And let You in

See
I had been dying
For some fresh air

College
Ames, Iowa
Surrounded by cardboard cutouts
All those lost souls

THE LAST LOVE LETTER

Blindly following life's instructions
As broadcasted on BET
The "learning" channel

People who check This Box
Talk like This
Dress like This
Wear these shoes
Listen to This Music
Dance like This
Think Like This
Want This
Like This
Dislike That

There is This
Folks
And This is all

We'll get back to you
When This changes to That
So that you can keep current
With the trends

Lest you perish

Stay Black

Ames, Iowa
Tripping over clones
Of characters off rap videos
NBA Basketball and NFL Football Players

Everybody had to be a baller
A pimp
There were no consequences
They were going to "The Show"

Street poets and intellectuals
Deep, precious things
Erykah Badu
love jones
Maya Angelou
Everything so abstract
So heady
What the fuck are you talking about?
Do you even know?

Christians and Muslims
Let's all get saved
Renounce our devilish ways
'Cept that
I kind of liked my devilish ways
Pass me that J

Frat boys
With their precious little letters
And their dog collars
Barking around the party
Naked
Naked and utterly fucking ridiculous

Everybody
With their pretty little labels
Jackets with special colors

THE LAST LOVE LETTER

Cafeteria tables

And then there was You
Glorious You

You stood apart

I checked Your collar
No tag
You didn't seem to have a label

And I loved You
Right from the start
I suspect

Do I resent You
Because I gave You some pussy
And You didn't care about me?

No
I don't think that's it
(ok...maybe just a little...I might resent You just a little...but I'm working through it...slowly but surely)

I fucked You
Because I loved You
Loved who You seemed to be
That first night

So much like my fantasy

I continued fucking You
Despite the bullshit
The reality of the whole thing
Because I loved You
Loved who I thought You *could* be

You could be my fantasy

I wanted to be close to You
In that way

Specifically
In
That
Way

Cuz You were
My living dream

I touched my dream

In bed
Was
The only time
I was
Ever
Real
With
You

The only time

THE LAST LOVE LETTER

Rubbed Your pretty little head
Arched my back
And let You see Me
The Real Me
My True Secret Self
Who Loved You

Loved You

With a Fiery Love
A Fiery Love Without Pride

No
Flowery words
Not my specialty
Not at that time

Or ever
Matter of fact
I've always been better
With vinegar than honey

You're right
I didn't say the sweet, soft things
You liked to hear
I never batted my eyes
I was never coy
And I never acted right
When You were near
You had Your fantasy too
I know

But I touched You
Sometimes
(More often than not)
Like You were a God
And I
Your Worshipper

On my knees
Worshipping You

There wasn't a sweet, soft thing
I hesitated to say
To You
With my hands
My lips
My tongue
With all of me
During sex

Not one

I deluded myself into believing
You heard
My version of sweet, soft things

You rested Your pretty little head
On my chest and in my lap
To hear my fingertips whisper
"I love You"

It's probably more likely
You just wanted a hand job

THE LAST LOVE LETTER

I suppose
With someone
You actually like
You're fabulous in bed

Roman candles
Fireworks
Ecstasy
Orgasm
The whole nine

FABULOUS
I'll bet
Wouldn't know
(For future reference…fucking someone…for whom You feel so much disdain…such as myself…doesn't bring out The Lover in You…so You know)

We can't help who we like
I know

I just wish
When You picked a woman
To elevate above me
To place on a pedestal
In my face

To show me
Who I should have been
To have Your Love and Respect

Because You did
Often
Rub my face in it

And, yes
I do understand
No worries

Interesting
Yeah
That's the word

Interesting to see emotions so strong
They can't be hidden behind a mask

And
I AM
The Master of the Mask

Powerful
To watch a person wilt
As You shine on another
Seemingly oblivious

I know
That's one from my playbook

Interesting
Like burning ants with matches
It's interesting

THE LAST LOVE LETTER

Here's a secret
You would have been better served
If You had picked one
That had honored You
As much as I did

When I let You in

Without making You jump
Through Hoops of Fire
Like a trained seal

I thought
You were
Better Than That
Cooler Than That
More Real Than That
Like we could just skip the bullshit
The games
And all that

Get right to the part
Where we saw each other
For who we really were
And we appreciated
The Real
The Suffering
In one another

Cuz I saw You
I saw Your suffering

Living in two worlds
Never quite belonging to either
Never quite belonging at all
And where was Your guidance?
Making Your own way

And I thought You were so beautiful
Broken and beautiful
Fucked up and familiar

But I was wrong

Seems that happened
From time to time

I didn't know You

I didn't know
You liked to jump
Here Boy

And chase dust bunnies
That every time
You got too close
Blew away

Into the arms
Of someone else
Who made Her jump
And chase too

THE LAST LOVE LETTER

Someone
Who made Her
Work for it

Right?
That's the model
For demure, feminine conduct?
Right?

Took the fun out of it
Didn't I?
By not pretending
To be indifferent
About You

Game-playing
The most mature approach
To a relationship
I agree
Nothing like withholding
To build trust and openness

See how beautifully it worked for us?
(Be calm…I'm using the term "us" loosely here)

You're right
I should have
Instead
Refused to take Your phone calls
And gave You some lame excuse
Because I didn't want to be bothered
Smothered
By all Your love and attention

That's what I heard
She did

That's what I heard

And it provoked
A loving response
From You

That's what I heard

She didn't answer Your calls
And You snapped

You snapped
And She let You go

She let You go
And then You lifted Her up
Up to Her pedestal

Tell me it's not true

You
Not God-like at all
Just human
Wanting someone
Who didn't want You

Do You ever think
That maybe
She acted like

THE LAST LOVE LETTER

You made it too easy for Her
Because She loved someone else?

Do You ever think
Even if You had made it hard
She wouldn't have put in the effort
Regardless
Because She loved someone else?

Did You ever think
That maybe
A Girl
Too Good
For anyone in Des Moines
According to You
(That's what I heard)
Might just have been
A Lovesick Puppy
Chasing after a man
Who didn't see Her?

Much like myself
With You

Like me with You

Cuz I assure You
All the ones that I never fucked
Whose phone calls I avoided
And then left
When they snapped
While trying to endear myself to You
Think I shine brightly too

Up on my pedestal

Like a Star
Brilliant
me
Dream Girl
'Magine that

Choosing not to fuck someone
Not so hard to do
You know
If you just don't see them

It's not Virtue
Darling
It's called Disinterest
Feel free to credit it as that

And don't get me wrong
I thought She was shiny too

I mean
She *did* have that one neat trick

Didn't have a damn thing going for Herself
But She barely saw You
Ta-da

Mystifying
To me too

THE LAST LOVE LETTER

And I don't write this to hurt You
Not now
Not in my Last Love Letter
(ok…maybe just a little…I might be trying to poke You just a little…but I'm working through it…slowly but surely)

Here's some perspective

We only chase
The ones
Who run away

We only value
Those
Who don't value us

When we don't value us

I know

Crazy
Hard to see the sense in that

Bet with Her
Suzy Shine
You would have been FABULOUS
An unselfish lover
Considerate and kind

Would have taken Her to The Club Yourself
Big entrance
On Your arm
'Stead of just meeting up there

You'd put Your arm around Her waist
All night

If She let You

If Her boy wasn't around
And his boys weren't around
I'm sure She'd let You

All the pretty girls would know
You were
Officially
Off the market

She'd be in Your car
At the end of the night
And there would be no doubt
She was leaving with You

You'd have given Her hungry kisses
Loud kisses
Savored those kisses on Her lower lip

Whispered with Your fingertips
"*I love You*"
As She laid Her pretty little head
On Your chest and in Your lap

You would have waited
Waited for Her
In bed
And You would have come together
FABULOUS

THE LAST LOVE LETTER

Miss Shiny
Your Dream Girl
'Magine that

I'm sure You have

We can't help who we feel
Who we get into
Or who we don't
I know

For too long
I believed
My mistake
Ruined my chance
With You

My mistake
Cuz You were there too

If memory serves
Dropped Your drawers pretty quickly too

And I forgot to hold it against You

Then
Like Five Seconds Ago
It occurred to me
Maybe
Just maybe
It wasn't so severe a transgression
That whole "Sex on the First Date" thing

Hear me out

I remember
Long ago
Kale
My favorite lover in Ames
Dated a girl
For an entire summer
Who he fucked
In the back of a car
Outside of a party
Couple hours after they met

Hell of an introduction
If I say so myself

The entire summer

Got that little Fun on the Farm Fact
From a mutual friend
Who was explaining
Why I didn't hear from Kale
The entire summer

The entire summer

What was even more fascinating
Was when he basically stopped seeing me
The NEXT summer too
To hook up with the sow
Again
Though she was pregnant
With someone else's kid

THE LAST LOVE LETTER

(So weird…how quickly I just typed that…like nothing…I reminisce…my lover and his pregnant snatch…holy shit…I'm over that one…well, I'll be damned…feather in my cap)

Point being
For the few
The few who have chemistry
Maybe trust
(I don't really know the "formula"…actually…
never been one of the few)
That, alone, doesn't sink the battleship

Maybe
You just didn't like me

There's a thought
Huh?

I always had a life in Ames
A life full of other lovers
Other loves
Other heartache
More despair
And I had some fun too
I'm not gonna lie
I'm sure
You're well aware

You might not know this

I loved Kale
With my whole heart
I loved him

Though he wasn't a perfect fit
(Actually, he wasn't even a good fit…I see that…now…blinded then…clearly seein' it now)
He was a better fit for me
Than You

He wasn't threatened by me
First and foremost

We talked
Kale and I

We tried to understand each other
Weren't always successful
But we tried

He was fearless
Young and fearless

He expected good things for himself
And me too

I didn't remind him
Of everything he wasn't
Of everything he wouldn't be

Confident and secure
He didn't require
That I validate him
By parroting everything he said

THE LAST LOVE LETTER

He realized I was a person
My own person
A different person
Different mentality

Separate and unique
Not just some extension
Of him
Simply existing
To make him look good
I was never a trophy

He wasn't defined by my conduct
Didn't feel the need to change it
Didn't try to control me

Hold me down
Teach me
Punish me

He didn't feel like he was competing
With my accomplishments
With my dreams
With who I was
With who I wanted to be

I didn't have to hide my sunshine
From Kale

He wasn't threatened by me

You
My Love
You were threatened
And pretty easy to offend

I did a hell of a job at that
Threatening and offending You
Even when I wasn't trying

Especially
It seemed
When I wasn't trying

Like walking on eggshells
It was
Lots of the time
As a matter of fact

Remind me
When I do start dating again
That men
Boys
Who start our conversations with
"I'm just a regular guy"
Are not for me

See
In the beginning
They're so cool
Non-threatening
Witty
So disarming
Laid back
Bullshit with anybody

THE LAST LOVE LETTER

Regular guys
They're fine

'Til I start talking
About wanting to write a book
Share one of my dreams
Then it's find-something-wrong-with-me time

So that they don't feel so
You know
regular

Love
Doesn't feel like that
A competition
I don't think

Maybe I don't know

I stayed in my world
My world
Where everybody dreamed big
And colored within the lines
Safe

You stayed in Your world
Your world
Where people went to work sometimes
Or they just lived off their stripper girlfriends
Safe

Time passed
The anger subsided
Then came the craving

I craved You
Living in my world
Where everybody looked the same

I craved You

Craved kissing Your face
Your beautiful, beautiful face
Kissing You everywhere

I could feel Your shadow
Like a feather on my lips

Rubbing my hands through Your hair
Massaging Your scalp
Your coarse hair
Under the pads of my fingers
You would move Your head from side to side
With Your eyes closed
You'd help me out

The weight of Your body on top of mine
When You were asleep
You pressed against me
As I wrapped my thighs around Yours

See Your smile
Hear Your laugh
Your voice in my head

THE LAST LOVE LETTER

They haunted me
These things
These memories
Snippets of happiness
With my living dream

I craved You
In an undeniable way
My parade of lovers
Never quite taking Your place

I craved You
More and more
Each day

There was no getting around that

I'd reach out
To You
My Love
Against my better judgment

And get my hand smacked

Hypnotic mantra
Running through my head
All the time
Like a chant

I cannot be the only one who loves
I cannot be the only one who tries
I cannot be the only one who gives
I cannot be the only one who cries
I cannot do it all alone
I am not like her
I'm not hard-wired for that
And maybe
Maybe
He's just not worth it

I used to have this fantasy
Walking into a bar with Kale
Hand-in-Hand
Finally
Having Gotten Our Shit Together

Kale and I
Hand-in-hand

And in this bar
Were all the girls
All his girls

The ones that hated me
Who sneered or laughed
Or talked shit
They were all there
Watching us

Kale and I
Hand-in-hand

THE LAST LOVE LETTER

And my friends
His friends
Non-believers
Never thinking that we could make it
Watching us

Kale and I
Hand-in-hand

And all the guys I had ever been with
Were there too
Watching us

Kale and I
Hand-in-hand

And as I scan the crowd
Feeling good
Contented
Next to my man

I see You

Looking at me

Next to my man

And I drop his hand

Always hated that You
The One who never really got me
The One who could take me or leave me

On any given day
Could ruin my happily ever after
Just like that

Yeah
I've read all the books
It's a problem
I know it's a problem

The familiarity
Right from the beginning
Was always a problem

Too familiar
You were

The experts
They speak to me
Through their books
And in my head

They say

My fixation with You
Is a vain attempt
To win the love
I was denied
As a child

I'm just a lost little girl
In a body with tits
Able to grant carnal wishes
Playing the same sad, old movie in my head

THE LAST LOVE LETTER

And You
You are the embodiment of
My bitter, critical mother and
Distracted, emotionally unavailable father
All wrapped up in a beautiful package
Bearing a freakish resemblance to my little brother
So familiar

YOU ARE
An unhealthy obsession

I gravitate towards You
Though I stand a snowball's chance in Hell
Of actually getting my emotional needs met
To avoid more appropriate romantic relationships
Out of fear
An irrational terror
And a sick, twisted habit
Of only chasing the ones who run away

I AM
Scary and Damaged
Blah blah blah

Don't get me wrong
This may very well be true
It's even probable
Very probable
I'm imagining
It's actually the most likely
Of all scenarios

But it doesn't erase
When I saw You
First time in three years
Driving a black car
On 63rd Street
7:40 A.M.
Going to work
I assume
Grinning and waving at me
Not mad at me anymore
My smile was huge
Huge

Because I couldn't help myself

You feel good to me
After everything
You still feel good to me
My rational mind might say one thing
But my heart consents to You

My heart consents to You

Before I have time to think
To remember
I feel good

When I see You
The first feeling
Is a kind of bliss

I am standing
Exactly where I need to be

THE LAST LOVE LETTER

For one perfect moment
The whole world is a beautiful place
Because of You

The bad thoughts
They come after

When I stop feeling
Stop following that beautiful bliss
With another blissful thought
About You
And I start thinking
Purposefully veering off course
Pulling up
Connecting
The bad thoughts
Ugly memories
Of You

I think the bliss scares me

Then
I start hating You
For dropping me

Blaming You
For breaking me

Amanda Easton
Cracked and Broken
Because of You

Why didn't You ever just say it?
"Amanda, I'm not interested"

You acted that way
And You were so direct
About everything else
I was certain
So certain
At any moment
You were just going to say it
You were going to release me
With those words
Thankfully
"Amanda, I'm not interested"

I needed to hear it
From You
From Your lips

It could not be implied

I wouldn't have denied it
If it had ever actually been expressed

But You didn't say it
You never said it
All those years

And I asked You
More than once
I gave You Your chance

I believed You

THE LAST LOVE LETTER

I believed that You liked me
Just a little

I believed
You left the door open for me
Just a crack

Even after all that

And I resented that
That little chance
You might have given us
Cuz it was little

Just a crack

Because there wasn't a banner
Bearing my name
Across Your door

As if I deserved that

You told me once
I only saw my side
I didn't see Your side

I saw Your side
I want You to know
I've always seen Your side
(Wasn't exactly in love with Your side though…so You know…there was no sympathy for me on Your side…and very little seeing of my side going on…on Your side…so You know)

That first night
At Roadhouse Ruby's
When we met
(For the second time)

I was out
With a group of guys
Who were best friends
With Kale

Yep
Out with his friends
Gave You my number

Our first date
You came to my dorm room
I had a picture of my high school boyfriend
In a frame

Fucking You
On our first date
While seeing Kale
With a picture of my high school boyfriend
In a frame

In the morning
I left You
Laying on the couch
To go to class

Told You not to answer the phone

THE LAST LOVE LETTER

Nothing as appealing as a girl
Out with her lover's friends
Who gives You her phone number
And fucks You
On the first date
Under the watchful eye of a high school boyfriend
Who might call the next morning
While she's at class

And that was just the first night

Believe me
I understand

And it burns
It burns
It burns

Nothing about the way we started
Would have given anyone
Anyone with any sense
The impression
We were meant to be anything
Anything more than sex

I understand why
You were so angry with me

I always understood
All that time

I understood
Throwing pencils and elbows
Ultra-shitty behavior
But I understood

I demanded love from You
Arrogantly
Loudly
Angrily
Petulantly
I demanded it

As if it was my right
When I had no right to that

You
You were supposed to
Love me back
First and foremost

You were supposed to make
Loving You
Feel safe for me
That was Your job
In my head

Make it stop
Make this stop
Feeling so much like quicksand

That was completely in Your power
In my head

THE LAST LOVE LETTER

And You owed me that
You owed me that
Because I gave You some pussy
Because I anointed You King
God of My World

You didn't give me
The Love
The Security
The Gratitude
I was due

Open season
On You

Often
I've lashed out
On You
Quite often

I've judged You
Harshly
My Love

My Mirror

My friends
I get it

I had a fling
With Kale's roommate
Roommate

(Right…take a second…read that again…not just a friend…oh no…
they *lived* together…a crime punishable by death in Amandaland)

I was always pissed at Kale
For one reason or another

He paid attention to me
The Roommate
The way my friends paid attention to You
So attentive

I'd call
Kale'd be gone
With some other girl

He would talk to me
The Roommate
Made it better
For about half a second
(he's the guy who told me Kale complained that I kissed too hard…an opinion…and not a flattering one at that…all those girls *and* unflattering opinions…I let The Roommate make up his own mind about my kisses…and other stuff too)

I did it
Of course
To be
Vindictive

Sick as this sounds
It actually made me feel closer to Kale
Cuz screwing some random nobody was nothing

THE LAST LOVE LETTER

He might not even hear about that
That would feel
Dangerously like
Moving on
Which was not the point of the exercise
And a waste of time

The Roommate
Could not go unnoticed
That
That would have impact

My friends
I get it

(I do want You to know this though…I never fucked anyone to spite You…did it to others…I never did it to You…I fucked people, in spite of the fact that I preferred Your company over anybody else's in the world …now, I *flirted* with other people to spite You…that I did)

And the phone
Not big on it
I never call anyone
I never call anyone back

If they're mad about that
The callers
They've kept it to themselves

They still speak to me
Respectfully

And they don't hold grudges
I don't think

Like I did
With You
For being the exact same way

I always returned Your calls though
I just wanted You to feel the same way
Tried to punk You into feeling the same way
Sorry

I'm sorry
For the times I screamed at You
In public
Unnecessary and disrespectful
We didn't owe each other anything
Only now am I aware of that

And I was very intolerant
Of You being loud
Or critical
Toward me
Which wasn't fair

I'm sorry
For the time
We were having an unpleasant phone conversation
And the phone accidentally disconnected
My thanking God
And just not calling You back
Thank you God
(It did disconnect accidentally…I swear)
So rude

THE LAST LOVE LETTER

I'm sorry
For the time I called You
To make plans
So that we could see each other
Getting it all set up
And then never calling You back
Gives the impression that I'm flaky
Unreliable

Which is sad
Because I'm neither flaky nor unreliable
When I'm involved with someone
I really like
(I want to explain that one…I call You…You don't know where You and Your friends will be that night…You want me to call back…and I said I'd call back…so I should have called back…but then I got to thinking about why You didn't just invite me to Your house…You know…like we could all just meet at Your house and go out from there…I thought that if You were driving all the way up to Ames to see me…and I didn't know what my plans would be…I'd just invite You over…so that You'd know…regardless, the night was about seeing You…but You didn't…and there could have been a lot of reasons for that…You didn't suggest it as an option and I never asked…I just got the feeling You weren't that interested…so I didn't call back)

I'm sorry
For interrupting You so much
I never let You get a word in edgewise
Talk, talk, talk
That's all I did
I talked over You
Like what You had to say
Didn't matter

Certainly wasn't as important
As my next thought

In my defense
I was always really nervous around You
When I get nervous
I get chatty
Super chatty
Which is a shame
Cuz I hung on Your every word
I remember practically every word

I'm sorry
For turning my back
And walking away from You in public
If You didn't act just right
Or say the exact right thing

Or sometimes
Just because

To maintain the illusion
That I was still in control
Of myself

I was in control
And You didn't really matter

Though You were the person
I left the house to see

You were always the person I left the house to see

THE LAST LOVE LETTER

Right now
I'm thinking about letting people see us
The real us
How we really live
That's hard
Terrifying actually
(For me anyway)
Especially
If you don't trust the person
Or their good opinion matters
For whatever reason

Right now
In this instant
I understand

I'm so out of balance with life
(You should see my house…if You did…You would know…beyond a shadow of a doubt…I'm so out of balance with life)

And being crushed
Under the weight
Of grown-up responsibilities
So many things
So many
I'm just not good at

Doggie-paddling
Barely keeping my head above water

And I have no intention
Or desire
Whatsoever
Right now
In this instant
To let anyone see what's behind the curtain

Building a mystery

Especially not You
Whose good opinion
Matters
Matters most of all

That night
You let me come home with You
After the bar

Cuz my ride left without me
Cuz I had been sitting in Your car
For 45 minutes
Talking to You

Pretty pissy
You were

And I get it

You had no intention of taking me home that night
You just wanted to talk to me
In private
So that I wouldn't make a scene
About You and My DiDi Baby

THE LAST LOVE LETTER

You didn't know I hadn't driven to Des Moines
Until it was too late
Until my ride was gone

I put You in a tough spot that night
Rudely declaring
That I was Your responsibility
Because I was sitting in Your car
At the end of the night

I was my responsibility
That night
And always
Not Yours

My anger suggested
You didn't even have a choice
About taking me home with You
That night

I realize that now
Having my own messy place
And being so out of balance with life
A lot like You
I think
At that time

I intruded on You and Your home
That night
With my pushiness
With my arrogance

And Instead of just respecting Your space
Where You were kind enough to let me stay
And appreciating Your trust
Your enormous trust
That night
For even letting me in
I cleaned it

I cleaned it
Though I specifically remember
Before You left for work
You telling me
Not to go through Your shit

I went through Your shit
Like I was Your Mom
And I cleaned it

I cleaned it
Cuz having a warm, comfortable place to sleep
On a night when I was ass out
Completely of my own making
Wasn't good enough

It also had to be spic and span

And I wondered
Bitterly
Why
You rarely invited me over again

THE LAST LOVE LETTER

I thank You
For being a friend
To me
That night
Cuz You were
My friend

Fuck
I'm sorry

I needed You
To be
The One

I realize that now

And what You needed
What You wanted
Who You really were
Didn't matter

I needed
That's all I knew

Like a child
I thought
What I needed
I could only get
From You

See
I had fantasies
About my Perfect Guy
He had Your face
Your body
He looked just like You

And he was
Everything

Witty
Funny
Clever
Sharp as a tack

He lived in two worlds
Street *and* Refined
Like a mix between a wolf and a Burmese cat

Vulnerable and Guarded

Open and Impenetrable

Generous With Praise and Justifiably Critical

Spontaneous and Conservative

Regal and Humble

Personable and Precious

Vain and Deserving

THE LAST LOVE LETTER

Intoxicating

Like a breath of fresh air

In my fantasy
In my dream
I would open the window
And let Him in

And he would wash away
All my sin
With a fiery love
A fiery love without pride
Without prejudice

I have yet
12 Years later

To reconcile myself
With my past

Still not ok
With that time
When I was 18, 19, 20
And not a butterfly

When all I ever really wanted to be
Was a butterfly
Light
Free
Pretty
God, I wanted to be pretty
And shiny

You were going to make me pretty
Make me shiny

You Majestic Creature

Your love was going to make me pretty
Make me shiny

And wipe me clean

Never happened
My redemption

And I've resented You
Ever since

Your side
Am I right?

For what it's worth
I was so scared
So scared of You
Terrified
More scared of You
And Your judgment
Your rejection
Than anything or anyone
In this world

I had done it before
Looked foolish before
Felt silly before

THE LAST LOVE LETTER

And ashamed before
I had lost
Before

Hard to be open
When you know what you're risking

Not so easy to bounce back
And I had lost
Lesser men than You
I've actually never been good at bouncing back

Had this very real feeling
After loving You
And losing You
Inevitably

I would Never
Really ever
Get me back

The Real Me
My True Secret Self

Amanda Easton
A Goddess
With her little face stuck in the mirror
But a Goddess nonetheless

Buried in You
Somewhere

Lost
In the crowd of broken hearts
Just holding my place in line

Lost in Dead Moines

Being nonchalant
I thought that would save me

I don't care
I don't care
I don't care
I don't care
Tonight, I don't care

It could be true
Maybe
With practice

As misguided as it all was
The purpose
Was self-preservation

Now I realize
Trying to protect myself
I just half-assed it
I half-assed my chance with You

I read somewhere once
There's no such thing
In life
As "maybes"

THE LAST LOVE LETTER

There's just indecisiveness

You either want something
    Or you don't

You either move toward something
    Or you don't

        I asked June
        The Psychic
        About You
        Cuz I didn't know
        Hoped she knew
        If You were worth it

I should have known

        That
        That is my one regret

        Kale
        I decided was worth it
        Rolled the dice
        And lost
        But I don't look back

        Kale and I
        We tried
        To be lovers and friends

But we thought about things differently
    Felt about them differently
Wanted different experiences from life

It didn't work out
And it was nobody's fault

Kale and I
After everything
We're good

Follow your bliss
That's what they say

I'm stuck
Like a block of salt
Frozen
Looking back
At You

I never did
Follow my bliss
In any real way
Not with You
And now I'm stuck

My life moves along
Like a train on a track
Ghost train
Cuz I'm too busy staring at a door
That's closed

A door that closed long ago

Trying to figure out how to pick the lock
Not knowin' if I want to pick the lock

THE LAST LOVE LETTER

Choosing to wait
Instead
Hoping someone better comes along
Someone more like me
And less like You
Then never actually giving anybody a chance
I don't even bother to clean up

Startin' to feel safe
Staring at that door

Stuck

Stuck on You
My Love
My Beloved
My King
My Superman
My Fantasy
My Living Dream

It's time to let go
I know

I can't carry this anymore
All this baggage

My planet of regret
It's heavy
And I'm so tired

It's time

Hating You
Blaming You
Obsessing over You
And what went wrong
Strategizing
How to win You back
Playing that same sad, old movie in my head

Trying to capture that love
That love I never had

Just keeps me here
Stuck

I'm going to try
Right now
Something different
Because I'm lost
Completely off the map

I'm going to try to put
Two good thoughts
About You
Together
In a row

Follow my bliss
Find the road
And move on

Things will be different
I know

THE LAST LOVE LETTER

When I put
Two good thoughts
About You
Together
In a row

Two more thoughts
Good ones
Will come to me
I know

It's time
To kiss You goodbye
And let go

I've loved You
From the first moment
I saw You

Loving You
Is the only thing
I've ever done
Consistently
In my whole fuckin' life

Showing You
That love
All that love
I've never done anything
Less consistently

And I've blamed You
All these years
For not making me feel safe
So that I could love You
And receive my redemption

So I could forgive me
Finally
For all those bad choices

And my shifty behavior
Made it unsafe
Like quicksand for You too
I know that's true

My mother says I look back on my childhood
And I only remember the bad stuff
I never remember the good stuff

So don't take it personally

It's programming
For survival
Emotional survival

Now
It's Automatic

This
I'm actually very practiced at

THE LAST LOVE LETTER

The strategy
Has been
To be vigilant
About remembering the bad times

Until I didn't have to be vigilant anymore

Cuz they were right there
All the time
Guiding my actions
I filter my entire life's experience
Through that lens
It's automatic

I've kept my finger on the trigger
Just in case something bad
Tried to creep up
On me
Again

Of course
Something bad
Will happen
The world is a bad place

I was ready
I am ready

Ready…steady…bam
Laid it down

Nothing surprised me

Nothing bad surprises me
Anymore
Enrages me
Yes
Surprises me
No

Belief and expectation combined
Powerful
The power to create worlds
In belief and expectation combined

Trust no one
And you will find no one
Worthy of trust

Got to work on this strategy
Cuz the intention is to feel less
To preempt feeling

Not workin' though
I just feel more
And it comes faster
With my finger on the trigger
Looking for the bad

I find more to hate
And my rage rises even faster

THE LAST LOVE LETTER

I'm killing anything I might love
At the first sign of imperfection
Out of fear

It's all happening
Almost automatically
Anymore

I've created these bad things
With my focus
With my attention
With my belief
With my expectation
With my behavior

Even now
I know
Things would be different
For us
If I thought well of You

I suspect
I project
My own thoughts
That I might be unlovable
Off on You

You
Are more than just a pretty boy
I fucked in college

You are The One
The One who sees through me

Past the caramel skin
The big tits
Pretty smile
The long hair

The great sex
Interesting conversation
Insightful moments
Nuggets of truth I share

My cherry-red SUV
My condo on the west side
The degrees
My big job
My consulting business
My $100,000 a year

All that good shit
That good, glittery shit
That blinds them all

You know
Not everything that glitters is gold
You know

You see
None of it really matters
Cuz deep down
I AM
Scary and Damaged

THE LAST LOVE LETTER

Unlovable

I'm more scared
Of being loved
Than of never being loved at all

The latter
I expect

You told me once
You were afraid to succeed
It's why You didn't try

We have that in common

You see me
The Real Me
My True Secret Self
Unlovable

And I hate You
I hate You

The hatred
Binds me
To You

My quest
Make You love me
Make me lovable

Keeps me from moving on
Spend all eternity
Punishing myself
For not being good enough for You

I could stop
Right now
I'm still breathing
I could stop
Take this very second
Turn this all around

I could stop playing the victim
And You'd stop being the villain
In my tale of woe

Could stop
Trying to prove to myself
That I am
Worthy of Love
Just because You think so

You
The One
Who doesn't even know me

Made You
God of My Little World
And You don't even know me

Could right now
Stop focusing on You

THE LAST LOVE LETTER

Remove You from the equation
And just declare myself
Lovable

But it would feel like a lie
Feels like a lie

Which is crazy
Cuz if You look it up
Amanda means "lovable"
My birthright

Worthy of love
Am I?

Loving me enough
There's the work that's left to do

Could finally just accept
This whole "unlovable" thing
Has nothing
Nothing to do with You

My problem
Mine alone

And You
You are just the unlucky bastard
I happened to screw

So…
Let that be a lesson to You

Some of us are easy
Happy Little Carrots
Bouncing 'round
Whorin'
Without a thought in our heads
Easy

And some of us are slightly deranged
Gorgeous girls
Who give good love
Looking for our Daddy
In every stranger
We touch
Every stranger
We fuck
Waiting for the inevitable disappointment
Two seconds away
From the next temper tantrum
Crazy

You might want to find out
What's what
Before You jump in bed

That was a joke
Not funny?
I thought it was funny

I can put
Two good thoughts
About You
Together
In a row

THE LAST LOVE LETTER

Because I can remember the good stuff
I remember the good stuff too

Our first date
We walked around Ames
And we talked
For hours
Actually had a good time
Before the sex

You were exactly how I wanted to be
Who I wanted to be
Real
Raw
Intense
Vulnerable

You were lost and confused
But You were honest
You didn't pretend to know the way

I just wanted to wrap my arms around You
Keep You safe
You were so fuckin' honest
It was the sweetest thing

That night
You kissed me
Even though I had strep throat

And You left me a note
Taped to my dorm mirror
The next morning
Even after we had sex on our first date
Even after that shit about not answering the phone
It was signed "Thy Sweetheart"
Your note
Which was just really cute

We talked that time on the phone
About my feelings for You
You said You understood
You didn't think I was crazy
(well, You did think I was crazy…but not like crazy crazy)
You said
You liked me too

And You let me come over
That one night
When I had my hair in cornrows
Even though I showed up at The Club
With two guys from Des Moines

Cuz if that had been me
Watching You
Walk into The Club
With two girls from Ames

There would have been no discussion
About who You were there with
And how it seems You do shit
To hurt me
Without even thinking

THE LAST LOVE LETTER

I
Would have spent
The entire night
Pretending like
You didn't exist

Poof
Who?

So thank You
For being a bigger person than me
As strange as that night was
With the arguing
And the tension
It was cool
Talking to You
Having a moment with You
My Love

And You gave my Dad
Those uniform patches for his collection
While I stood at the door
Of Your job
And barely acknowledged
What a Profound and Beautiful thing
You had just done

You were a nice guy
You had shitty moments
You were moody
Me doing my "bitch" routine
Probably didn't help
But all-in-all
You were a nice guy

And not for me

I'm sorry
For everything
I'm sorry

I am

I see You
And not with rose-colored glasses either
I want You to know that

I see You
Clearly

I think
You are
A regular guy
With regular friends
Regular interests
And regular ambitions

You live a regular life

And
I think
You are
Incredibly exceptional too

I miss You

I miss You

THE LAST LOVE LETTER

I miss kissing Your face
Your beautiful, beautiful face
Kissing You everywhere

I miss rubbing my hands through Your hair
Miss Your coarse hair
Massaging Your scalp

I miss the weight of Your body on top of me
When You're asleep
(that one time I moved You off of me…I did that to be mean…I too can be passive-aggressive after sex…and I'm sorry)

My little King
My beautiful King

I miss Your smile
I miss Your laugh
I miss the fact that despite everything in Your life
That must have gone wrong
You are eternally young
Eternally hopeful
Eternally willing to laugh

I miss Your sarcasm
Your wit
Sharp
My Love
Sharp as a tack

I miss Your grace
Your generosity
Your kindness

I miss Your huge, huge heart
The way You forgive
And You try to forget

I miss watching You
Work the crowd
Radiating warmth

The way You treat people
Like Royalty
Like maybe they're not
Lesser mortals
After all
Not to You anyway

You shine on everyone
Anyone
Dazzling Rays of Your Sunshine
Like a spotlight
The Winner

We all need a little sunshine

I miss the way You manage
To lift everybody up
To a pedestal
In some way

Including me
When I deserved it
On one of my better days

THE LAST LOVE LETTER

And most of all
Most of all
I miss that little crack
That itty bitty crack
In Your door
For me
Now that You've gone away

You didn't say it
That You weren't interested
That You didn't want me
Because it would have hurt me
And You were just trying to avoid that
Toward the end

I see that now

Thank You
Thank You for being my friend

I love You

I LOVE YOU

And everybody says it
But nobody ever means it
I've said it
And not meant it
Probably ever

I mean it
Wholeheartedly

I love You

You know how I know?

Your ultimate happiness
I suspect
Has absolutely nothing
To do with me
Nothing at all
I'll bet

In fact
I know

And I want that happiness
For You

Anyway

Desperately so

For You
My Cherished One
I will always want good things
The best things
For You

My Mirror
My Love

THE LAST LOVE LETTER

For You
I wish for more rainbows
Always
Many more rainbows

I wish that for You
My Love

And me too
Me too

You and I
We tried
A little something

But we didn't have anything in common
We lived in different worlds
We weren't the least bit compatible

I understand
You did what You did
Cuz You didn't want to feel
Less than

Please understand
I did what I did
Cuz I only wanted to feel
Good enough

It didn't work out
And it's nobody's fault

You and I
Finally
We're good

On that note
I'm off
To find a cleaning lady
A good babysitter
And a horse

I'll see Ya
Sometime
On the road

Be well

Sincerely,
Amanda

P.S. So…here's my book…after all…thank You…
thank You for the inspiration…and Happy Belated Birthday.

Printed in the United States
97855LV00006B